Starwhal

To Peter - Keep sparkling!
M.R.

To my very own star - Julia
T.B.

HODDER CHILDREN'S BOOKS

First published in Great Britain in 2020
by Hodder and Stoughton

© Hachette Children's Group, 2020
Illustrations by Tim Budgen

A CIP catalogue record for this book is available from the British Library.

ISBN: 978 1 44495 436 4

1 3 5 7 9 10 8 6 4 2

Printed and bound in China

MIX
Paper from
responsible sources
FSC® C104740
FSC
www.fsc.org

Hodder Children's Books
An imprint of Hachette Children's Group
Part of Hodder and Stoughton
Carmelite House, 50 Victoria Embankment, London, EC4Y 0DZ

An Hachette UK Company
www.hachette.co.uk
www.hachettechildrens.co.uk

Starwhal

Written by **Matilda Rose** • Illustrated by **Tim Budgen**

Hodder
Children's
Books

Next time you're in fairyland, make sure you visit Mrs Paws'
Magic Pet Shop in the town of Twinkleton-Under-Beanstalk.
It's a truly enchanting place. There are flying piglets,
cute baby griffins and even pugicorns!

One day, Millie the Mermaid came
to the Magic Pet Shop, looking for
her perfect magical pet . . .

"Those cats look cuddly," said Millie.

But the cosmic cats did not like water!

The baby dragon was so cute. But - *splash* - out went its flame!

And - *splosh* - the talking llamas were not impressed with their soggy new hair-dos.

Would Millie ever find the right pet?

"Don't worry!" smiled Mrs Paws. "I've just had a special delivery . . ."

It was a creature with big, round eyes,
cute, flappy flippers and a long, twisty horn.

"A narwhal!" gasped Millie.

"Almost!" laughed Mrs Paws. "This is a **starwhal**. She's very rare. Just one touch from her magic horn will make anything sparkle!"

"Oh, I love her, thank you!" said Millie.

"Starwhal's magic can do amazing things," said Mrs Paws. "You just have to learn how to use it in the right way."

Back home in Coral Cove, Millie made sure
that Starwhal had everything she needed:
a comfy bed, toys to play with and plenty
of delicious sea-puffs to eat.

And she couldn't wait to try out
Starwhal's magical powers.

With a single touch of
Starwhal's horn . . .

Poof! The bed was
covered in sparkles.

Poof! The wardrobe
was full of twinkling,
glinting outfits.

Poof! Millie's whole bedroom was
transformed into a starry, shimmering wonderland!

"Please could you make my bubble-blower sparkly?" asked Millie's brother, Milo.

But Millie remembered what Mrs Paws had said. She must use Starwhal's powers in the right way.

"No," said Millie. "I must only use Starwhal's magic for important things."

But later Millie couldn't resist using a little more of Starwhal's magic:

Poof! The Singing Rock was all twinkly.

Poof! The seashell path shimmered brightly.

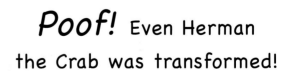

Poof! Even Herman the Crab was transformed!

And word soon spread through Coral Cove . . .

"Please could Starwhal
make my mirror twinkly?" said Lola.
"No," said Millie. "Starwhal is *my* pet
and I must use her magic wisely."

"What about my necklace?" asked Archie.

"Or my hairclip?" asked Pearl.

"Sorry, but I said no,"
huffed Millie.

But, back home, Millie decided to try out just a little more of Starwhal's magic for herself . . . and soon the whole house was glinting and gleaming!

It was so sparkly and pretty that Millie just *had* to show it off.
So she sent invitations to all of her friends:

You are invited to
a Starwhal Sparkle Party
Tomorrow at 3p.m.
Seashell Cottage, Seahorse Walk,
Coral Cove

Love, Millie X

Millie prepared an iced bubble cake and mixed up a jug of sea-fruit fizz, she polished Starwhal's horn and put on her best necklace. Then she waited . . . and waited . . .

But nobody came.

Millie's eyes felt hot and tickly. "Where is everyone?"
She sighed. "Come on Starwhal - let's go and find them!"

Halfway through the coral reef, Millie and Starwhal heard a funny *sniff-sniff* noise.

"Look! It's Prince Tristan!"
gasped Millie. "What's the matter?"

"I've – *sniff* – lost my – *sniff* – crown,"
Prince Tristan sobbed. "I'm supposed to be opening
the new Coral Cove Library this afternoon.
But how can I without my crown?!"

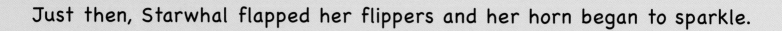

Just then, Starwhal flapped her flippers and her horn began to sparkle.

"Starwhal wants to help!" squealed Millie.
"I suppose we could use just a bit of magic . . ."

Millie picked some seaweed, plaited it and – *poof!* – Starwhal
transformed it into a sparkling crown!

"Thank you!" said Tristan, with a huge, happy smile. And you know what? His smile made Millie feel happy too.

Mrs Paws was right – Starwhal's magic *could* do amazing things if you used it in the right way!

Together, they swam to the library . . .

. . . just in time for the grand opening!

Tristan cut the ribbon, wearing his beautiful new crown.

And, to make the day extra special, Millie shared Starwhal's magic sparkle with everyone.

Library

"I'm sorry," said Millie to her friends. "No one came to my party because I tried to keep Starwhal's magic for myself. But there is more than enough for us all!"

Everyone went back to Millie's
cottage for the Starwhal Sparkle Party.

And soon Millie and Starwhal were having a wonderful, sparkly time
with their friends, in the most magical place under the sea: Coral Cove.

Because sometimes kindness is the best magic of all.